I read this book all by myself

....

To Jake, with love – RS
To Gabriella and Fabio – VP

A Red Fox Book

Published by Random House Children's Books
61-63 Uxbridge Road, London W5 5SA

A division of the Random House Group Ltd
London Melbourne Sydney Auckland
Johannesburg and agencies throughout the world

Text copyright © Ragnhild Scamell 2001
Illustrations copyright © Valeria Petrone 2001
Sunflowers by Vincent van Gogh © National Gallery, London

3 5 7 9 10 8 6 4 2

First published in Great Britain by Red Fox 2001

Published in hardback by Heinemann Library, a division of
Reed Educational and Professional Publishing Limited,
by arrangement with Random House Children's Books

Printed in Singapore by Tien Wah Press

THE RANDOM HOUSE GROUP Limited Reg. No. 954009
www.**kids**a**trandomhouse**.co.uk

ISBN 0 09 941733 2 (paperback)
ISBN 0 431 02409 X (hardback)

Jake and the Red Bird

Ragnhild Scamell   Valeria Petrone

RED FOX

Miss Greensleeve's class had studied sunflowers long and hard. They had touched them and sniffed them and counted their seeds. They had sown them and grown them.

How many seeds did yours have?

857.

The famous painter, Vincent van Gogh, loved painting sunflowers.

Everyone in the class had written a letter to him. Jake's letter said:

21 The Balconies
Fairtown FT19 8LQ

6 April 2001

Dear Vincent,

I was very sorry to hear that you cut your ear off. It must have hurt a lot. Was it because people didn't like your paintings? I like them a lot. When I grow up, I'm going to become a famous painter, like you. Today we are off to a gallery to see one of your sunflower paintings.

Lots of love from
Jake
XXX

On Tuesday morning the class lined up. They were off to the picture gallery, to make a drawing in the vibrant style of Vincent van Gogh.

I've forgotten my green pens

You can mix yellow and blue.

Emily led the long
snake of children. Close
behind her walked Jake
with his felt-tip pens
and sketch pad.

A gallery lady led them straight to Vincent van Gogh's painting of a vase with sunflowers. "These paintings are priceless," she said. "Make sure you don't touch them."

Jake felt she was looking directly at him.

The sunflower painting glowed like a fine jewel. "Feast your eyes on those vibrant colours, children," said Miss Greensleeve.

Look at those yellows!

Soon everyone was sitting on the floor.
Jake handed round the paper.

Most of the children drew
sunflowers.

But Jake drew a red bird. He pretended
that his felt-tip pens were artists' brushes
and that he was painting his bird with thick
paint. Just like Vincent van Gogh.

The red bird was sitting in a green bush.

Jake tilted his head trying to decide
exactly where to put the red bird's eye.

There!

The red
bird blinked.

Then it flapped its wings.
And before Jake could do
anything about it,
it had flown off.

Left behind was its white shape in the green bush. Like a missing piece of a jigsaw puzzle.

Emily's jaw dropped.

How did you do that?

"How are you two doing over there?" called Miss Greensleeve.

"All right, Miss," said Jake, hiding his picture.

Emily elbowed him.

Over by the van Gogh painting, something vibrant and red fluttered up and down. Luckily, Miss Greensleeve didn't seem to have noticed.

Jake and Emily sauntered across to the painting, trying to look as if they were studying it. Jake grabbed at the bird, but it slipped through his fingers and settled on one of the sunflowers.

Emily covered her eyes, murmuring something to herself.

"It's all my fault!" said Jake.

Come back!

23

Jake held up his sketch pad. But
the red bird ignored it.

"Creep up behind it," he whispered
to Emily. "I'll stand here
twittering."

Tweet, tweet, tweet...

"Emily!" called Miss
Greensleeve, sharply.
"Do not touch."

"But, Miss . . ." said Jake. "My bird is eating that sunf . . ."

"What?" Miss Greensleeve came running. Her face was purple with anger. "Who drew that bird?" she asked.

Jake held up his sketch pad.

"Me, Miss. Look."

Miss Greensleeve glared. First at the white bird shape. Then at the painting.

"I shall have to go and get help," she yammered, and rushed out of the room.

Don't anybody move!

The class stood as if nailed to the floor, staring as Jake's vibrant bird hacked away at the sunflower.

Emily tried to reach it.

29

The red bird fluttered down
behind the yellow vase. It sat there,
peering out at them.

Suddenly, Jake had an idea.
He drew a small pile of birdseeds.
That did it. The red bird flew
straight back to the green
bush on Jake's pad.

31

And while the red bird pecked at the seeds, Jake drew a golden cage around it.

He had only just finished when Miss Greensleeve came charging back with six gallery people.

33

Everyone looked. First at Vincent van Gogh's picture. Then at Miss Greensleeve.

"It's, it's . . ." stuttered Miss Greensleeve.
The gallery people shook their heads.

35

Jake held up his sketch pad.

"Some people!" said someone.
"Good boy," said another,
patting Jake's head.

When they had gone, Miss Greensleeve
told Jake to give her his sketch pad.

Did Vincent ever have trouble with his paintings, Miss?

And all the felt-tip pens.

They were to stay in her bag for now.

And Jake and Emily were to keep up with

the rest of the class.

As they walked around the gallery, Jake thought of another letter he was going to write to Vincent van Gogh.

Dear Vincent,
Did any of your pictures ever leap off the page?...

40

But that was as far as he got.
Because, suddenly, he
heard a flutter. And
something vibrantly red
floated out of Miss
Greensleeve's bag.
It was a feather.

As Jake bent to pick it up, Emily elbowed him again.

The vibrant red bird in the
golden cage had started to sing.

Jake and Emily are having fun with colours. What can you find out about red and green?

Experiment 1.

1. Photocopy or trace the bird below twice. Colour one red and the other green.

2. Look at the red bird for 30 seconds, then look at a piece of blank paper. What colour is the bird now?

3. Look at the green bird for 30 seconds, then look at a piece of blank paper. What colour is the bird now?

I forgot my red pen. Can I mix two colours together to make red?

Experiment 1: green: red
Experiment 2: the green bird is in the cage.
Experiment 3: the bird looks like it's moving.
Speech bubble: no, red is a primary colour.

Experiment 2.

Look at the red bird for 30 seconds again. Then look at the cage. What happens?

Experiment 3.

Colour the area around the red bird bright green. Then look at the bird. What happens?

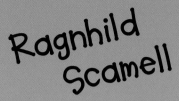

Meet the author.

Ragnhild Scamell

How did you get the idea for this story? I was just about to get up one morning and there it was. That's what ideas usually do. They arrive when you least expect them to.

How long did it take to write this story? It took quite a long time, because I like to change things as I go along. At first, I thought maybe Jake drew a dog that hopped into the sunflower painting. But the dog knocked the vase over and spilled the water and got Jake into too much trouble. So a red bird seemed just the thing.

Have you ever seen the real van Gogh sunflower painting? I've seen the one in the National Gallery in London, and once, I went to the Van Gogh Museum in Amsterdam. Van Gogh painted about eleven sunflower pictures and they all sparkle with colour. A reproduction is good, but seeing those thick brush strokes for yourself is truly magic.

Can I write books like you? All you need is imagination, a piece of paper and a pencil. Or, if you are good at drawing, you can draw a story without words. Try it.

Valeria Petrone

Meet the illustrator.

What did you use to paint the pictures in this book? I used a computer with a special pen and pad. I prefer to work on pictures one at the time, one after another with no interruptions so I can concentrate better. It probably took me about two months to finish this book.

What gives you good ideas? Different things give me good ideas – going to the cinema, going on holiday, seeing friends, going for a walk around town . . .

Did you draw when you were a child? I used to draw all the time, even at school when I wasn't supposed to. I was often told off for this, but my teachers got used to it.

What did you like to do when you were little? What did you hate most? I loved reading in bed, going to the seaside, and playing football. I never liked getting up early to go to school.

Will you try and write or draw a story?

Can I be an illustrator like you? Yes, if you like drawing very much. You have to enjoy it, because an illustrator draws all the time, every day!

Let your ideas take flight with
Flying Foxes

All the Little Ones – and a Half
by Mary Murphy

Sherman Swaps Shells
by Jane Clarke and Ant Parker

Digging for Dinosaurs
by Judy Waite and Garry Parsons

Shadowhog
by Sandra Ann Horn and Mary McQuillan

The Magic Backpack
by Julia Jarman and Adriano Gon

Jake and the Red Bird
by Ragnhild Scamell and Valeria Petrone